MY MUM always LOOKS After ME

So Much!

MY MUM always LOOKS After ME So Much!

Sean Taylor

Frances Lincoln
Children's Books

David Barrow

We're going to the doctor.
I've got to have an injection.

The doctor is nice.
But I can think of things
that are *more* nice.
Like toys.
And bananas.

Mum says I'm going for an injection
because she has to look after me.
But that's the problem, really.

My mum always
looks after me *so much*!

Like, she always tells me
I've got to eat broccoli.

Then whenever I sneeze,
she puts another jumper on me.

And now she says I've got to have an injection.

I don't mind *too* much.

Gorillas are brave,
even when we're small.
Normally we don't even cry.

The doctor is nice, like usual.
She says, "What flies and wobbles?"

The answer is...
A JELLYCOPTER.

So it's a joke
    as well as an injection.

And it does hurt a little.
But...

...because I'm brave, the doctor gives me this
stick thing that she uses to look at your tongue.
It smells like strawberries smell.

I
LOVE
my stick
thing!

It's good for flicking!

And balancing!

And just sniffing!

Oh NO!

My stick thing!

It smelled of strawberries!
I liked it.

But Mum says it won't
take long to actually go
back and ask if I can have
another stick thing.

The doctor is even more nice.
Look what she's given me!
And this one is better...

It smells like BANANAS!

My mum always
looks after me *so much*.

Brimming with creative inspiration, how-to projects, and useful information to enrich your everyday life, Quarto Knows is a favourite destination for those pursuing their interests and passions. Visit our site and dig deeper with our books into your area of interest: Quarto Creates, Quarto Cooks, Quarto Homes, Quarto Lives, Quarto Drives, Quarto Explores, Quarto Gifts, or Quarto Kids.

My Mum Always Looks After Me So Much © 2019 Quarto Publishing plc. Text © 2019 Sean Taylor.
Illustrations © 2019 David Barrow.
First published in 2019 by Lincoln Children's Books, an imprint of The Quarto Group,
The Old Brewery, 6 Blundell Street, London N7 9BH, United Kingdom.
T (0)20 7700 6700 F (0)20 7700 8066 **www.QuartoKnows.com**

ISBN 978-1-78603-181-5

Illustrated digitally
Designed by Zoe Tucker
Edited by Kate Davies
Published by Rachel Williams
Production by Kate O'Riordan and Jenny Cundill

Manufactured in Dongguan, China TL112018
1 3 5 7 9 8 6 4 2